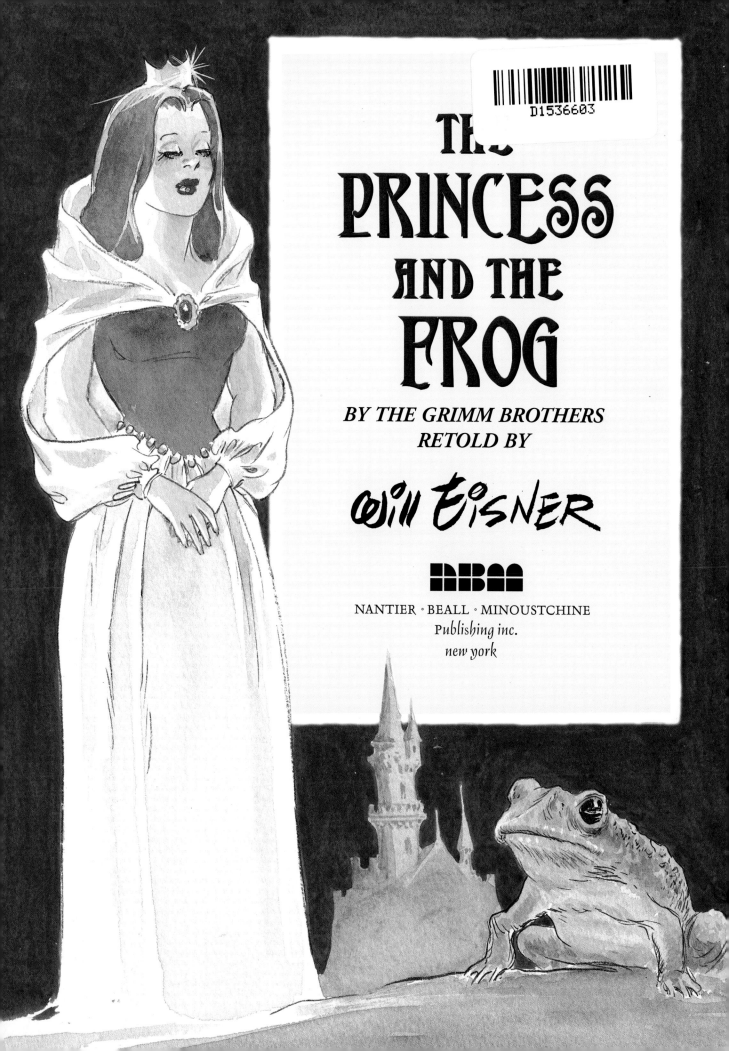

THE PRINCESS AND THE FROG

BY THE GRIMM BROTHERS
RETOLD BY

Will Eisner

nbm

NANTIER · BEALL · MINOUSTCHINE
Publishing inc.
new york

Other adaptations by Will Eisner:
Moby Dick, $15.95 hc, $7.95 pb
Sundiata, $15.95 hc, $7.95 pb
The Last Knight, $15.95 hc, $7.95 pb
Other adaptations:
The Wind in the Willows, vols. 1-4, $15.95 each
The Fairy Tales of Oscar Wilde, vols. 1-3, $15.95 each
The Jungle Book, $16.95
Fairy Tales of the Brothers Grimm, $15.95
Peter & The Wolf, $15.95
($3 P&H 1st item, $1 each addt'l)

We have over 150 graphic novels in
stock, ask for our color catalog:
NBM, dept. S
555 8th Ave., Suite 1202
New York, NY 10018
www.nbmpublishing.com/tales

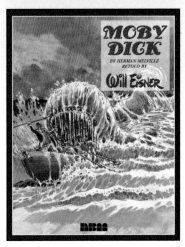

©1999 Will Eisner
ISBN 1-56163-346-1, paperback
ISBN 1-56163-244-9, clothbound
Printed in Hong Kong

5   4   3   2

THE PRINCESS AND THE FROG
BY Will Eisner

ONCE UPON A TIME... IN A FAR OFF KINGDOM BY THE SEA ...

THERE LIVED A HANDSOME YOUNG PRINCE

AHH, MY PRINCE, HERE IS YOUR LIST OF DUTIES FOR THIS DAY.

THANK YOU FAITHFUL HENRY ...PERHAPS ONE DAY I'LL BE KING AND I'LL SERVE THE KINGDOM.

BUT TODAY I MUST **ONLY** DO THE SIMPLE DAILY AFFAIRS OF THIS CASTLE.

HOW MODEST AND WISE! NO WONDER THAT YOU ARE LOVED BY ALL.

1.

6

AND SO... THE PRINCE (FROG) LEFT HIS CASTLE AND WENT OUT INTO THE WORLD

BUT IT WAS NOT SO EASY TO FIND A PLACE... FOR AS YOU KNOW NEW FROGS ARE NOT EASILY ACCEPTED IN A POND WHERE THEY WERE NOT BORN.

WELL YOU KNOW HOW MEAN FOLKS CAN BE TO NEWCOMERS.

GET OUT OF HERE... WE DON'T WANT STRANGERS HERE!

SO HE WANDERED FROM POND TO POND... WITH NO LUCK! UNTIL, AT LAST, ONE DAY HE CAME UPON A WELL.

AH... THIS IS THE ONLY PLACE LEFT FOR ME!

7.

AND IT HAPPENED THAT THIS WELL WAS ON THE GROUNDS OF A WEALTHY KING'S ESTATE.

... EVERY DAY THE DAUGHTER OF THIS KING—A LOVELY PRINCESS—WOULD ENJOY PLAYING IN THE GARDENS NEAR THE WELL. HER FAVORITE GAME WAS TOSSING AND CATCHING A BALL OF PURE GOLD.

8

12

THE VERY NEXT DAY...
AS THE PRINCESS SAT AT DINNER WITH HER FATHER THE KING....

16

18

AND INDEED THE PRINCE AND PRINCESS SOON RETURNED TO THE KINGDOM-BY-THE-SEA., WHERE THEY MARRIED TO THE GREAT JOY OF THEIR PEOPLE.

BEFORE LONG THEY BECAME KING AND QUEEN OF THE REALM WHICH THEY RULED WITH GREAT KINDNESS AND WISDOM.

FAITHFUL HENRY REMAINED AT THE KING'S SIDE

AND FOR HIS DEVOTION FAITHFUL HENRY WAS APPOINTED KEEPER OF ALL CREATURES LARGE AND SMALL. ...UNDER HIS COMMAND HE DECREED ALL FROG PONDS WOULD BE FOREVER PROTECTED AS A NATIONAL TREASURE.

AND THEY LIVED HAPPILY EVER AFTER